The Junior Novelization

Adapted by Irene Trimble

Based on the screenplay by
Andrew Stanton & Jim Reardon

Random House New York

In Memory of Rick Trimble
—I.T.

Published in the United States by Random House Children's Books, a division of Random House, Inc., New York, and in Canada by Random House of Canada Limited, Toronto, in conjunction with Disney Enterprises, Inc. Random House and colophon are registered trademarks of Random House, Inc.
Library of Congress Control Number: 2007938147
ISBN: 978-0-7364-2502-5
www.randomhouse.com/kids/disney
Printed in the United States of America
10 9 8 7 6 5 4 3 2 1 First Edition

In the vast regions of outer space, beyond the twinkling lights of a million stars, a murky, smog-covered Earth floats lonely and silent. The deepest oceans are all but dried and gone. What had once been blue sky is now a dust-choked brown that can still look almost golden when sunlight filters through it.

Beneath the thick atmosphere that surrounds the planet, mountains still rise up through the haze, and once-great cities filled with vacant, crumbling buildings share the landscape with towers of trash, neatly cubed and stacked as far as the eye can see. Only one thing moves along this bleak twenty-ninth-century skyline.

Day in and day out, for more than seven

hundred years, he has worked to clean up the mess left by humankind. The scouring sands that sweep along the avenues seldom deter him as he thrusts his shovel-like hands into the heaps of trash and scoops it into the compacting unit in his chest. Once full, he closes the squeaky doors of his front panel, shakes a little, and produces yet another perfect cube ready to be stacked.

This is his directive.

It is what he has been programmed to do.

His name is WALL•E: Waste Allocation Load Lifter, Earth class.

He is a robot.

He is dented, dirty, and rusted . . .

And he is about to change the entire world.

"Chirrrp!" A little cockroach jumped happily onto WALL•E's shoulder. As the toxic winds began to pick up speed, WALL•E and his only companion motored bouncily toward home. WALL•E's treads were wearing thin, and the cockroach held on bravely as they crossed the rough terrain.

Over miles of desolate waste, WALL•E saw buildings and highways and rolled across the remains of broken bridges. Everything was branded with the same logo: BUY-N-LARGE. BnL had its stamp on everything. The megasuperstore had once overseen almost all operations on the planet.

As WALL•E hurried onward, he rolled over an old newspaper. TOO MUCH TRASH! EARTH COVERED! BNL CEO DECLARES GLOBAL EMERGENCY! the headline proclaimed. WALL•E did not notice.

He passed a salvage yard full of other rusted WALL•E units, shut down long ago. The cockroach watched eagerly as WALL•E stopped to examine something of interest on one of the old units—its treads.

The treads were thick bands of rubber, built to protect the WALL•E units' metallic wheels like giant tires. This old unit's treads were in much better shape than WALL•E's.

WALL•E quickly switched his old pair for the newer ones as the cockroach chirped and jumped excitedly. Then, moving on, WALL•E felt the cockroach settling happily on his shoulder, enjoying the new, smoother ride.

WALL•E rolled past a BnL billboard, activating its holo-graphic message as he moved. The image buzzed to life. Several loudspeakers began broadcasting the chipper voice of a human announcer, recorded centuries ago.

"Too much garbage in your face?

There's plenty of space out in space!

BnL star liners leaving each day.

We'll clean up the mess while you're away!"

WALL•E headed across a bumpy freeway overpass, activating another ancient billboard. Through the smoggy haze, the image of a sparkling BnL star liner flashed onto the screen. Its happy passengers appeared to be enjoying all the amenities of a luxury cruise ship.

"The jewel of the BnL fleet: The *Axiom*!" the announcer's voice boomed. "Spend your five-year cruise in style. . . ." But the people had been gone from Earth far longer than five years.

"The *Axiom*!" the voice exclaimed proudly. "Putting the 'star' in 'executive star liner.' "

The wind was starting to howl now. WALL•E squinted and turned on a set of tiny windshield wipers to clean the lenses of his eyes. Looking across a bay that had dried up long ago, he saw a battered old BnL truck. WALL•E's spirits rose.

WALL•E picked up his pace as he headed toward his truck. He scurried up and pulled a lever on the truck's side. Slowly the back began to come down, and WALL•E happily sped up the ramp and into the trailer. Home!

The wind whipped the truck as WALL•E peeled his new rubber treads from his wheels. He would put them on again in the morning before returning to work. But now it was time to relax. He removed a battered BnL cooler from his back. It was his collection box, and he was ready to begin the nightly ritual of going through the treasures he had found in the trash during the day.

But first, WALL•E went to an old television set and turned on his favorite video: *Hello, Dolly!* He always played it when he arrived home. After watching the video for a minute, he turned back to press a button that activated the rotating racks of shelves where he neatly stored his treasures. The day had yielded some very special finds: a few old toys and utensils (all of which made WALL•E curious, since he didn't know what they were) and a lighter.

As he listened to the background music from the video, WALL•E perked up. He moved among his many treasures, stopping often in front of the fuzzy images scrolling across his television screen. The actors were singing and dancing to the song WALL•E had been humming all day. He paused, waiting for the next part. When it came, he hit the Record button on his chest and moved closer. WALL•E could see that the actors were not dancing now. They were walking together and looking into each other's eyes. Then they took each other's hands.

WALL•E tilted his head, his large eyes gazing

tenderly at the screen. He interlocked his own two robotic hands. And for a moment the lonely robot wondered what it would be like to hold someone else's hand.

Later that night, when the storm had ended, WALL•E rolled outside and turned over his collection box to clean it out. He pressed the Play button on his chest and listened to the song again. Although the little robot wasn't programmed to understand romance, it was romance that pulsed through his circuits. It was this same strange impulse that made WALL•E gaze up at the few stars visible through the polluted haze and wish for someone to share his world.

Suddenly, WALL•E's internal systems gave him a warning sign. The wind was picking up again. WALL•E checked the horizon. A massive sand-storm was approaching across the dried-up bay.

WALL•E swiftly headed back into the truck. He was familiar with the dangers of being caught in a sandstorm—air so clogged with dirt and debris that he wouldn't be able to see; whipping winds that would fill every crevice in his robotic joints with sand; and, of course, the chance of being buried. This time he was lucky: he was close to the safety of his truck.

A blinding wave of sand roared closer as WALL•E entered the truck and began to raise its door. He stopped for a moment, remembering, and then turned and made a robotic noise—like a whistle—to call for his cockroach. The door shut just as the storm hit, with both master and pet safe inside their little home.

WALL•E unwrapped a BnL sponge cake and set it on a shelf. Still moist from the preservatives that had kept it intact for centuries, the little cake made a comfy cockroach bed.

WALL•E collapsed into a box shape and backed into an empty shelf. Rocking the shelf back and forth like a cradle, he closed his eyes and shut down for the night. Outside, the full force of the storm raged across the terrain.

"WARNING! WARNING! WARNING!" WALL•E's charge-meter light flashed at a dangerously low level the next morning.

"Mmrrr," WALL•E groaned. It was hard to wake up! Still groggy, he made his way outside and crawled up a ramp of trash to the top of his truck. Once settled, he opened his solar panels to the hazy sun. He stretched his tiny arms and felt a surge of power run through his little cables. Finally feeling awake, he heard his solar panel chime, indicating that his electronics were fully charged for a day's work.

WALL•E happily got down from the roof and fastened his collection box to his back. He was ready to head out to work. As he rolled down the truck's ramp, suddenly—*CRUNCH!*

Horrified, WALL•E realized that he had accidentally rolled over the cockroach! WALL•E moved away and stared at his pet's flattened body.

"Ohhhh," WALL•E whined. He looked down at his pet, searching for signs of life.

POP! The bug sprang up, happy as ever, and none the worse for wear! Relieved, WALL•E let his pet hop onto his shoulder for a ride and started out again.

The day began with the usual task a WALL•E unit would expect to perform on a desolate, trash-filled planet: compacting trash. But for WALL•E, the garbage contained treasures. Thinking beyond his robotic programming, WALL•E was always looking for new things buried in the trash—things that he could add to his collections. Had there been any other robots or people on the planet, they might have thought it was a bit odd for a bot to be interested in anything other than his predetermined directive.

Today a set of car keys caught WALL•E's attention. Not knowing what they were, he went about inspecting them. He pushed the remote lock button, and somewhere deep in the trash heap a car alarm chirped. That was interesting.

Next WALL•E came across a diamond ring in a little case. He closed the case with a snap. Open. *Snap!* Close. *Snap!* The case was fun! WALL•E tossed the ring back into the trash but carefully packed up the case to take home. He also found a rubber ducky, a bobble-head doll, and an old boot. They were definitely deserving of further attention—and possibly worthy of going into his collections.

He came upon a paddle with a ball attached to it by an elastic string. When he shook it, the ball rapidly bounced against the paddle. The bouncing action delighted WALL•E, until—*POP!*—the ball smacked him right between the eyes!

"Eee!" WALL•E beeped. He didn't like this thing at all. He quickly tossed the paddle aside and turned toward something else—a fire extinguisher, though WALL•E didn't know that. He simply saw something that was red and kind of heavy. WALL•E examined it until he found what he was looking for: a lever. Usually, levers activated something. WALL•E pulled it.

WHOOSH! The blast from the extinguisher propelled WALL•E into a loop-the-loop, spinning him over and over until he finally crash-landed in the trash. WALL•E moaned. He couldn't figure out what use humans had found for this shiny red object. Perhaps it had been some sort of game, but he didn't like it. Time to move on.

Digging and digging, WALL•E soon saw an old white refrigerator. He activated a welding beam between his large binocular-like eyes and cut the door down the middle. With a clang, the two pieces of the door fell off the refrigerator. WALL•E looked inside and saw a small green object in a corner. It was sprouting from a pile of dark brown soil. WALL•E gazed at it in wonder. Now, this was something really unusual. He didn't know why, but he liked it. The object had a stem with flat green ovals hanging from it. Gently, he picked it up. Making sure that it was safely cushioned in its soil, he placed it inside the old boot he'd found earlier. He tucked the object inside his box to examine later.

WALL•E sensed that the green thing was special. What he didn't know was that it was a plant.

Thrilled with his new treasures—especially the green object—WALL•E finally returned home at the end of a long day of work. He had just reached for the lever to open his truck when a dot of red light appeared at his feet. WALL•E stopped. He stared at the dot, then slowly reached down to touch it. The dot raced away along the ground. WALL•E scurried after it. The dot led him into the vast dry bay. WALL•E was so taken by the one red dot that he didn't notice the many other dots coming at him from all sides. The little laser lights formed a circle around him.

WALL•E heard a low roar in the sky. He looked up and saw what seemed like three hot suns coming in his direction! The roar grew louder and louder. Terrified, WALL•E felt the ground shaking. Columns of fire dropped from above and surrounded him on three sides.

WALL•E furiously started to dig a hole in the ground. He jumped into it just as an intense burst of fire scorched the earth.

As suddenly as the roar had started, things quieted down. WALL•E slowly raised his head and peeked out of his hole. Something very big was looming over him. He climbed out of the hole and banged his head on a metal object.

It was the underside of some sort of spacecraft!

With nowhere to hide, WALL•E made the best of what was available. He placed a small rock on his head, boxed himself up, and hoped he wouldn't be noticed. WALL•E wasn't used to visitors, so he wasn't sure what to expect. But his curiosity quickly began to get the better of him. He wanted to be able to see what was coming even while he remained hidden. Cautiously, WALL•E crept a bit closer to get a better look.

The spacecraft deposited a capsule on the ground. The capsule began to unfold, its exterior peeling away in sections. It was as if something precious were being unwrapped.

Then he saw her emerge—a sleek egg-shaped white probe-bot with gleaming blue eyes. WALL•E was breathless as he watched her hover gracefully above the ground. She was the most beautiful thing he had ever seen.

Her name was EVE.

CHAPTER 5

The spacecraft began to close up. A low hum filled the air. WALL•E suddenly remembered—he was under a ship! The hum was coming from the ship's engines, which were now roaring to life. It was time to take cover again. WALL•E dug another hole in the ground and jumped into it.

When the smoke cleared, WALL•E once again raised his head. He looked up and saw EVE. She was circling over the desolate bay. As she swooped and darted like a hummingbird, she emitted a blue ray from her front panel and scanned the terrain. WALL•E scrambled out of the hole and quickly found a boulder to hide behind. He watched EVE continue to scan random objects, occasionally doing a loop in the sky. She zoomed past

WALL•E's rock. Frightened yet enchanted, the rusty and dented WALL•E unit kept watching this sleek new state-of-the-art robot. This was love.

EVE gently descended to the ground, and WALL•E decided to move one rock closer to her. As he rolled forward, his treads loosened some debris—*RATTLE, RATTLE, KLUNK!*

EVE whipped around in the direction of the noise. She instantly raised and fired the blaster mounted within her arm. *KA-BLAM!* WALL•E's boulder exploded into bits. The shivering robot was unharmed but terrified.

EVE scanned the area again. All quiet, she noted, no signs of life. She moved on and wandered through WALL•E's vast avenues of trash. WALL•E rolled after her. She had just tried to blast him, but like a puppy, he continued to follow her, unable to stop.

He watched her scan a mound of tires. Then he flinched as his cockroach decided to approach EVE from behind. Her razor-sharp sensors picked up the movement. She spun and blasted the bug with a direct hit. Unharmed, the insect simply crawled out of the smoking crater and, with his usual curiosity, continued to approach EVE.

She let the roach get closer. The little bug intrigued her, and she let him crawl up her arm. WALL•E heard her emit a series of electronic beeps. She was giggling! The roach must have tickled her.

WALL•E's spirits soared. EVE had feelings! Then, just as suddenly, he was struck by fear again as EVE's sensor turned in his direction. She locked onto him with her scanners and fired rapidly with her blaster arm.

WALL•E dodged the blasts, scooting among trash piles as EVE obliterated them one by one. With nowhere left to hide, WALL•E boxed himself up and shook uncontrollably. EVE stopped firing. Her electronics hummed, "Identify yourself." But WALL•E heard only beeps and whistles. He didn't understand what EVE was saying.

She slowly approached the shivering box. The cockroach ran down EVE's blaster arm and hopped onto his master. EVE's blue light scanned WALL•E. NEGATIVE. He was not what she was looking for. She retracted her blaster arm and glided away.

Peeking out from inside his box, WALL•E watched her, completely awestruck.

As EVE continued her search, WALL•E followed her to an abandoned BnL store. EVE scanned the store, registering NEGATIVE, NEGATIVE, NEGATIVE.

But when she glanced back at the not-so-hidden WALL•E, the little robot panicked. Whirling awkwardly, he bumped into a rack of shopping carts, sending a noisy avalanche of carts down a flight of stairs. Unfortunately, WALL•E went tumbling and bouncing all the way down, too. Finally, the humiliating moment ended with a crash. The carts could move no farther, and neither could WALL•E. He was wedged between the carts and a pair of doors that refused to open. EVE ignored him. WALL•E began the slow process of untangling himself.

That evening, WALL•E climbed to the roof of the BnL power plant. He patiently waited, hoping to see EVE somewhere in the darkening sky. Suddenly, her blue light flashed on the horizon, and his tiny circuits skipped a beat.

WALL•E watched her come in for a landing, ready to shut down for the night. He waited, then moved toward her. Once, he accidentally tripped, but luckily the noise didn't wake her. Sure now that she was asleep, WALL•E crept closer. Carefully, he measured her dimensions with his robotic arms. Then, turning to a pile of trash, he began to weld, using the laser beam mounted between his eyes.

The next morning, EVE awoke to find a sculpture of herself made entirely of gleaming trash. Impressed, she rose and circled the egg-shaped sculpture. It had sparkling blue glass eyes, just like hers.

WALL•E watched her from behind a stack of pipes. He could see that she liked the sculpture.

Thrilled, he wanted to come out, but he hesitated . . . and the moment was gone. EVE glided away just as the pipes rolled down—*CLANK, CLANK, CLANK*—onto the happy little robot's head. Smitten as ever, he hardly noticed the extra few dents in his body.

EVE spent her day scanning the city. She scanned a car engine—NEGATIVE. She slammed the hood. A toilet—NEGATIVE. A space capsule—NEGATIVE. A freighter's hold—NEGATIVE.

And then something different happened: EVE got caught by the freighter's giant gray magnet! Swinging upside down, she flipped and wiggled every which way. But no matter how hard she tried, she could not free herself from the powerful magnet.

Shhhh-lop! She freed her body, but then her arm got stuck. When she freed that one, her other arm got stuck. Frustrated by her days of fruitless searching, EVE pointed her blaster arm at the magnet and blew it up.

She watched as the flaming magnet crashed through the deck of the freighter, causing it to catch fire and topple into the next freighter. Then another freighter toppled, too, like a row of falling dominoes. It was a gigantic mess!

Oooooo! WALL•E watched as smoke from the blast enveloped EVE. She was not only beautiful but powerful, too!

Then he cocked his head and looked at her again. She seemed different than before. She slumped. It looked as if she was ready to give up.

Cautiously, WALL•E—still blinded by love—climbed onto the other side of the anchor and very slowly inched toward her. Suddenly, she turned to him and hummed, "So what's your name?"

WALL•E was so shocked that he tumbled over backward.

EVE tried again. "Directive?" she asked. WALL•E was stunned by the sounds she was making. She was trying to communicate with him.

Even better, she didn't seem to want to use her blaster arm!

Though EVE spoke in a lovely hum, WALL•E could not understand a bit of it until he recognized the word "directive." Eager to connect with EVE, he loaded a pile of trash into his compactor and plunked down a cube for her. He struggled to speak, to let her know that this was his directive. "Di . . . rec . . . t—"

"Directive!" EVE interrupted sharply, helping him finish. His eyes grew large as he looked at her, wanting to know her purpose, too. But EVE hummed, "Classified." Her directive was a secret.

"Oh." WALL•E had hoped to learn more.

EVE scanned WALL•E's chest logo. "So what's your name?" she hummed robotically again.

Struggling to answer, WALL•E tried to form his beeping noises into the sound of his name. "WALL•E."

EVE nodded and repeated: "Waaaleeee." To the little robot, EVE's electronic voice sounded like music. He scooted a bit closer. "Waaa-lleee," EVE said again. Then she spoke her own name: "Eeeve."

"Eee-vah?" WALL•E said slowly.

EVE shook her head. "Eeeve, Eeeve."

WALL•E made the sound again: "Eee-vah!"

WALL•E heard her giggle. It was the happiest day of his life. He said it again, hoping she would giggle once more. "Eee-vah!" he said. "Ee—"

One of WALL•E's electronic warnings went off. The wind was whistling through the bay. A storm was coming—a big one. WALL•E reached for EVE's hand, but she pulled back, not understanding the danger of the situation. The sandstorm hit in a rush of swirling wind and debris. WALL•E collapsed into a box.

"WALL•E! WALL•E! WALL•E!" he heard EVE cry.

Through the blinding dust, WALL•E popped up from the safety of his box shape, reached out to EVE, and led her to shelter.

WALL•E pulled EVE inside his truck and closed the door tight. EVE looked around, intrigued by WALL•E's many collections.

WALL•E sensed her interest and proudly began to give her a tour. First, he handed her an eggbeater. As he looked for something else to show her, EVE spun the eggbeater faster and faster, until it whirled itself into pieces. Uh-oh. EVE quickly hid it, not wanting WALL•E to see what she had done.

But WALL•E had his mind on something else: the clear plastic wrap that had bubbles in it. Once again, EVE seemed delighted. He showed her how to pop the bubbles, then handed it to her and popped a few more bubbles encouragingly. She tried it, and then began a rapid-fire popping. In seconds, the entire sheet was deflated. This was fun!

And then WALL•E handed her his prized *Hello, Dolly!* videocassette—not expecting that she would pull the tape out of it! Emitting a high-pitched beep, WALL•E grabbed the cassette from EVE and carefully reeled the tape back inside. Terrified that it might not work, he inserted the cassette in his video player.

After an anxious moment of staring at his television, WALL•E saw his beloved characters appear on the screen, singing and dancing.

Relieved, WALL•E shuffled back and forth on his treads and mimicked the dancing for EVE. Extending his hand to the floor, he encouraged her to try, too.

EVE fell—*THUNK!*—to the floor and bounced back up again. WALL•E then tried a move he hoped would be less dangerous. He spun with his little shovel arms extended outward. EVE happily imitated him—but with a massive force that quickly sent her whirling out of control! *KLANK!* EVE accidentally propelled WALL•E into a wall of shelves. As he fell to the floor, his head clanged like a bell.

EVE gasped. One of WALL•E's binocular-like eyes was hanging loose.

WALL•E calmly reassured the distraught EVE. He felt his way through a pile of spare WALL•E-unit parts. Then he popped in a spare eye and brightly turned to EVE. Good as new!

As they continued exploring WALL•E's collections, EVE amazed WALL•E by producing a flame from an old lighter. As they stared at the flame, WALL•E realized he had never been this close to EVE. He looked up at her, the flame flickering between them. In the background, his favorite song from *Hello, Dolly!* played.

WALL•E reached for EVE's hand. Maybe now he could finally hold hands with her.

EVE turned to look at him, but WALL•E panicked and pulled his hand back, pretending to retrieve something from the floor.

Still, he wasn't about to give up. As EVE continued to stare at the television screen, WALL•E scurried off. There was one more thing that might win EVE's approval. It was the undisputed masterpiece of his many collections. He tapped her on the shoulder and held up the plant.

EVE's blue light immediately locked onto it. Her chest opened. WALL•E was shocked to see a tractor beam suddenly shoot from EVE's chest and envelop the plant. The beam had pulled the plant into a compartment in EVE's chest. Her panel doors slammed, and her system shut down altogether! Only a single green light remained pulsing on her chest.

"Eee-vah?" WALL•E said numbly. He shook her gently but got no response.

WALL•E panicked. "Eee-vah? Eee-vah!" he cried.

CHAPTER 8

The next morning, WALL•E pulled EVE up to the roof of his truck. He aimed her toward the sun and waited. But there was no change in EVE, not a single sign that she was recharging in the sunlight.

WALL•E took EVE to different places. He held an umbrella over her during a thunderstorm, and—*BOOM!*—the umbrella was struck by lightning. So was WALL•E.

WALL•E cared for EVE as she slept. When a sandstorm appeared on the horizon, he placed a barrel over her. He held the barrel steady as the sand buried him in a tiny dune.

After the storm, WALL•E had another idea. He decided that perhaps he could jump-start her electronic heart with his own. He attached the jumper cables, closed his eyes, and hoped for the best. But EVE's state-of-the-art electronic defense system was powerful and far more advanced than WALL•E's. *BOOM!*—the electric jolt toppled WALL•E.

A bit deflated but not defeated, WALL•E made a leash out of old Christmas lights, wrapped it around EVE, and whistled for his cockroach.

Pulling gently on the leash, WALL•E went for a walk with his two companions. Then WALL•E took EVE for a boat ride on a lake of steaming sludge. Using an old street sign as an oar, he rowed her to a particularly scenic scrapyard. He set her on the hood of a junked car to watch the sunset through the polluted air.

As he observed the light being refracted through the smoggy haze, the sky turned a brilliant purple and gold. To WALL•E, the worn and smoggy world he lived in suddenly took on a rosy glow. He sighed and etched WALL•E & EVE on an old post with his laser.

Later that night, WALL•E placed EVE on the roof of his truck, the solar Christmas lights around her aglow. He set up his television in front of her so that she could watch. But no matter what WALL•E tried, there was no response.

The next day, WALL•E decided to return to work. He halfheartedly got ready, then checked on EVE one more time. Leaving her on the truck's roof with the feeble hope that the sun's rays might awaken her, he turned away. Unenthusiastically, he called to his cockroach and set out.

At his work site, WALL•E noticed that he was just going through the motions of trash compacting. He was simply following his directive, like a normal robot. His passion for interesting items was gone. WALL•E realized he'd found the one thing in all the world that made being in it worthwhile.

WALL•E stopped and pulled out his lighter. Seeing it flicker, he sighed and remembered the good times he had shared with EVE.

A gust of wind suddenly blew out the tiny flame. WALL•E looked across the dry bay toward home. Was another sandstorm blowing in? No, it was something else: A bright glow was descending from the clouds. He heard the low rumble and instantly realized that it was the spaceship that had brought EVE. He raced toward home, terrified that the ship was coming to take her back!

"Eee-vah! Eee-vah!" WALL•E called out.

As he reached the freeway ramp near his home, WALL•E suddenly stopped short. In the distance, the probe ship was hovering over his truck. A giant robotic arm reached out and lifted EVE into the ship's hold.

"Eee-vah! Eee-vah!" WALL•E screamed as he scrambled toward her. The cargo doors closed as the rocket engines powered up.

WALL•E rushed down a hill of rubble and up a broken freeway overpass. Then, quickly, he stopped. He placed his cockroach on the ground and gestured to him: "Stay!" The disappointed cockroach sat down, chirping impatiently.

WALL•E careened toward the spaceship and latched onto it just as a wall of flame blasted from the engines.

Inside the ship, robotic arms fastened EVE into a slot among a long row of dormant probe-bots. EVE was the only probe-bot flashing a green light.

Outside, little WALL•E was steadily climbing the side of the ship as the final engines ignited. He clamped his small hands onto a metal support rod and closed his eyes as the rocket blasted into space. On the ground, WALL•E's cockroach dutifully stayed put as he watched his master disappear into the clouds.

CHAPTER 9

As the probe ship roared through the murky brown sky, WALL•E could feel the force of Earth's gravity on his body, pulling powerfully against the acceleration of the ship. He tightened his grip on the support rod as the ship burst through Earth's atmosphere. The engines slowed down, and WALL•E, now weightless, took in the majestic splendor of all the stars sparkling in clear space.

The probe ship passed the moon, where WALL•E saw a billboard reading BNL OUTLET COMING SOON! It stood in the lunar dust, forgotten long ago.

WALL•E blinked hard and recharged his solar panels as the ship zipped past the sun. Traveling quickly into deep space, the ship approached

Saturn. WALL•E reached out and ran his hand through the dust and ice particles that made up one of the planet's outer rings.

Mesmerized by the view, he saw a single light growing in the distance. He recognized it from the billboards he had seen on Earth. It was a gigantic luxury-class star liner. It was the *Axiom*!

The *Axiom* was enormous—wide and tall. At the lowest level, there was a garbage depot where the ship's trash was compacted and tossed into space. Just above that stretched loading docks and service-robot corridors. The next three levels were where the passengers lived: the least expensive economy-class units in the middle of the ship; coach class on the level above, with its main concourse (which looked like a huge shopping mall); and the luxury housing units overlooking the lido deck, high above them all.

The Captain and his autopilot also had a view of the lido deck from the bridge at the top of the ship. The bridge's control panels could activate practically anything on the *Axiom*—the Captain could broadcast announcements, adjust the fake sun that shone on the passengers (which gave them a sense of the time of day), and, of course, guide the star liner through space. One day, the Captain would look down on the lido deck and activate the holo-detector, a computer designed to confirm the presence of life on Earth. Then the great machine would rise from its platform and automatically take the ship back home.

As it approached the star liner, WALL•E's small probe ship was swallowed inside the *Axiom*'s docking bay, where it was locked safely into place.

Still clinging to the outside of the ship, WALL•E saw the loading dock come to life. From every corner, gleaming service robots of all sizes and descriptions appeared. Their names shining on their front panels, they paused until lines appeared in front of them on the floor. Apparently, the bots carried out their directives by following these preprogrammed lines around the ship.

The probe ship's cargo doors smoothly slid open, and WALL•E saw EVE. She was still shut down; only the green light on her chest was flashing.

"Eee-vah?" WALL•E whispered as a chrome-trimmed crane-bot lifted her out of the hold and lowered her onto the huge deck below. WALL•E was careful to speak softly and remain hidden.

Immediately, a squad of robots surrounded EVE. To them, she was Probe One. A tiny mint-blue robot with a bristle-brush head was beeping orders to the rest of the robots. His name was M-O. He was a microbe obliterator with one simple directive: clean.

M-O scanned EVE. Disgusted, he computed that she was fifteen percent contaminated with dirt. He signaled his crew, who hurried along bright red lines on the floor to begin the cleanup. A vacuum-bot, a sprayer-bot, and a buffer-bot zipped along their lines to do their jobs.

WALL•E watched as the crane-bot lifted one of the bots from the probe ship and lowered it onto the deck. WALL•E suddenly had an idea. He wedged himself into another probe-bot's place, and the crane-bot picked him up next.

As M-O continued to scan the probe-bots on deck, he suddenly came across WALL•E, who was boxed up and nervously trying to blend in. M-O turned to the boxed robot and scanned him: 100% FOREIGN CONTAMINANT! A red light popped out atop M-O's head and a siren began to wail.

Poor WALL•E, having spent centuries cubing trash, was very dirty indeed. M-O instantly charged at WALL•E in a cleaning frenzy. Frightened, WALL•E pushed him away with his front panel.

M-O tried again. WALL•E rolled backward, leaving a dirty trail on M-O's immaculate floor. M-O lunged forward and scrubbed at the track marks. Amused by his power over the cleaning-obsessed M-O, WALL•E had another idea. Just to see what might happen, he decided to stick out his tread and make another spot on the floor. M-O leaned over and scrubbed at it compulsively.

Teasing him now, WALL•E wiped one of his treads on M-O's head. M-O went crazy, trying to rid himself of the yucky stuff.

Suddenly, two steward-bots—the policing bots of the *Axiom*—emerged from a wall. Nearby, a small robot shot out of a pneumatic tube and into the docking bay. It was Gopher, the Captain's personal assistant. He quickly gave orders to the steward-bots. Then he headed toward the probe-bots. A blaring siren sounded, prompting the cleaning crew to snap to attention.

Gopher began to scan each probe-bot. He checked WALL•E and then moved on to the next robot. Realizing that something wasn't quite right, he stopped for a moment. He turned to look WALL•E over again, but the little robot was gone. Gopher continued until he finally came to EVE.

Gopher scanned EVE, and instantly, every alarm on deck began to sound. Green lights flashed everywhere. A hover transport glided up to Gopher. He beeped and ordered the crane-bot to lift EVE into the vehicle. Gopher climbed into the driver's seat and navigated the transport into an open elevator.

"Eee-vah!" WALL•E called, hurrying after the transport. He managed to hop inside the elevator just before its doors closed.

Behind him, the other bots began to file out of the loading dock. Each robot moved strictly along its designated line. M-O discovered WALL•E's latest filthy trail. But the dirt veered away from M-O's designated line, and bots were never supposed to go off their designated lines. Not ever.

M-O looked at his departing crew, then back at the dirt that irresistibly called to him. He closed his eyes and did something no service robot aboard the *Axiom* had ever done: He jumped off his designated line. Somehow, WALL•E had had a strong effect on the industrious cleaner-bot.

Cringing, M-O slowly opened his eyes. He looked around cautiously. No alarms. No whistles. Nothing had happened! That wasn't so hard, he decided, and cheerily began following WALL•E's tracks, scrubbing as he went. He was determined to find and clean this bot.

CHAPTER 11

Inside the transport, as Gopher patiently waited at the wheel, WALL•E could feel the elevator rising. An instant later, the elevator doors opened. WALL•E got his first look at the ship's robot passageway, which was located above the docking bay. Robots were zipping by at lightning speed.

Gopher smoothly turned into the traffic as WALL•E tried—and failed—to merge. He put one tread into the traffic and yanked it back, causing a pileup of mangled robots. Whoops! He heard multiple beeps of objection from the busy bots.

WALL•E was too frightened to move, but the transport carrying EVE was getting farther and farther away. Bravely, he decided to box up and try again. Disregarding all robot traffic rules and every designated line, WALL•E rolled toward EVE.

Weaving in and out of traffic, he spotted EVE on her transport up ahead. It was gliding toward an off-ramp. WALL•E chased the transport and suddenly emerged onto the deck above. Blinking, he saw the bright lights of the *Axiom*'s economy-class courtyard.

WALL•E noticed that the courtyard was surrounded by hundreds of guest rooms. Passengers filled the giant courtyard, reclining in chairs that hovered just above the floor. WALL•E looked at their faces. Humans had changed over the centuries. They didn't look like the photos in the old magazines and newspapers that littered Earth's surface. These humans were very large and very soft. Their legs had turned flabby from lack of exercise, and their necks didn't seem to exist at all.

WALL•E waved happily even though no one waved back. Moving forward, WALL•E tilted his head and saw the holo-graphic screens that all the reclining humans had in front of their faces. He noticed that what the humans lacked in leg strength, they more than made up for in powerful high-tech devices that provided them with information, fed them, and even moved them. The humans seemed bored and without purpose. Their world was completely digital. No one had any motivation to do anything. Bots served the humans' every need.

Still, WALL•E kept waving at them. He had not seen a human being in centuries!

Two passengers, John and Buddy, drifted by, boxed into their chairs with speakers on either side of their heads and holo-graphic screens in front of their faces. They could easily have spoken to each other directly . . . if they had had the motivation and ability to turn their heads and push aside the electronics surrounding them. Instead, they were isolated in the midst of a crowd of humanity, not even caring or knowing that they were right next to each other. WALL•E tried to follow and understand what they were saying.

"So what do you wanna do?" "I don't know. What do you wanna do?"

WALL•E saw Buddy's screen flash a virtual amusement park. "Let's ride the roller coaster again," Buddy said.

"Nah," John responded. "I've already ridden that a thousand times."

"Well, then what do you want to do?" Buddy asked.

"I don't know."

WALL•E left the arguing humans behind as he pursued the transport into a tunnel crowded with robots and more humans in hover chairs. For a moment, the screens connecting the humans flickered. The humans began to panic. They stopped talking and typed words like "Oh no, you're breaking up!" and "I can't hear you! I'm in a tunnel."

When the human passengers were disengaged from their electronics, it was frightening for them. But they quickly calmed down when the tunnel emptied into the star liner's main concourse. "You're back! I can hear you now!" the relieved passengers shouted. Their hover chairs glided across the main concourse.

The concourse was a city-sized mall. On the upper level surrounding the mall, WALL•E saw endless rows of guest suites.

He looked up, trying to take in his new surroundings. Everything was available to meet all the passengers' needs and desires—instant foods in the form of shakes, robots to give them massages and haircuts—but there was nothing that really drew the humans away from the holo-screens in front of them.

An announcer's voice suddenly filled the air. WALL•E jumped. "Happy *Axiom* Day!" the voice said, cheerfully booming across the deck. "Your day is very important to us! If you're not happy, you're not consuming!"

WALL•E didn't understand. He just wanted to find EVE.

WALL•E moved forward . . . and wandered across one of the lines on the floor. This broke the rules. He accidentally bumped into one of the passengers. Then WALL•E bumped into John, knocking him off his chair.

"Help!" John screamed, panicking. He didn't know what to do without his hover chair! He couldn't move! (Well, he could wiggle and scream, but he couldn't do much more than that.) The reclining passengers continued to glide by, not even noticing him. WALL•E lifted the helpless, overweight man into his chair. John stared at the strange bot. He settled into the cocoon of his artificial environment, but he would not forget the little robot who had just rescued him.

WALL•E saw Gopher driving the transport that held EVE onto a monorail packed with passengers. WALL•E maneuvered across the crowded floor, barely catching the monorail's last car.

WALL•E had to make his way forward through the cars to get to EVE. The monorail kept moving forward, too. As it zipped past dozens of themed restaurants in the food court, the smells of tacos and teriyaki wafted through the air. Service-bots shoved samples at the passengers.

"Mmmm, time for lunch!" the ship's announcer said. Instantly, large quantities of each specialty were served on every armrest.

The monorail passed a beauty salon where passengers were being polished and pampered. WALL•E heard the ship's announcer croon, "Feel beautiful!"

When the monorail rolled through the fashion district, everyone's screen suddenly flashed "Attention, *Axiom* shoppers! Try blue. It's the new red!" Within moments, the passengers' jumpsuits turned from red to bright blue. WALL•E looked at his own rusted exterior. It stayed its usual dirty brown.

WALL•E held on to the back of a seat as the monorail sped through a long tunnel. He was slowly making his way toward EVE.

But a human passenger named Mary blocked the way. She was chattering at her screen.

"Date? Don't get me started!" she said, annoyed. "Every holo-date I've been on has been a virtual disaster! If I could just meet someone who wasn't so superficial . . ."

WALL•E twisted and turned, trying to get around Mary, but she didn't seem to notice him.

"Him?" she said, completely unaware of WALL•E. "If he was any more into himself, you wouldn't be able to see his head."

Desperate to get to EVE, WALL•E pulled himself up onto Mary's headrest and speakers. They broke off. *Blink!* Mary's holo-graphic screen shorted out.

Mary was stunned. Her tiny but complex electronic system was wiped out. She looked from side to side, forced to take in the world around her. Astounded, she looked down and saw her own feet! Wiggling her toes, she adjusted her seat to an upright position to get a better view.

When Mary moved, WALL•E zoomed past her. But he didn't realize what he had done for her. From now on, she would experience life instead of having it served to her.

The monorail doors slid open and a voice announced their arrival on the lido deck.

A first-class tropical paradise, the lido deck was surrounded by dazzling white high-rise apartments and a plaza filled with sparkling pools.

Passengers reclining in their hover chairs followed the red lines onto the luxurious deck as Mary, the only passenger who was actually seeing it, rose to her little feet, stumbled forward, and exclaimed, "I didn't know we had a pool!"

The monorail glided across the lido deck, finally stopping at the entrance to the ship's bridge. Gopher drove the transport into the bridge's enormous lobby, where it stopped and beeped at the desk of a lonely typing-bot. A gate was lowered and the transport whooshed through.

WALL•E emerged onto the bridge and hid in the shadows of a huge circular room. The bridge was where the Captain and Auto, the *Axiom*'s autopilot and steering wheel, controlled the ship.

Auto seemed to dominate the room. With a large eye in the center of his wheel, he could view both the lido deck and deep space just outside the window. He had a long mechanical tentacle that he used as a hand to help him push buttons or lift things, and even lift objects periodically.

Gopher saluted Auto and presented EVE for inspection. WALL•E watched as Auto scanned EVE and began computing rapidly until a code blinked on his screen. Auto and Gopher exchanged several beeps and nodded.

WALL•E felt the floor beneath him move. Stifling a shriek, he realized—too late—that he was standing on a trapdoor. It opened to the Captain's quarters one floor below . . . which was exactly where WALL•E landed when he fell.

Auto, not noticing WALL•E, reached down through the hole right after him and activated the Captain's alarm clock. WALL•E boxed up in the dark room and hid.

"Captain," Auto said to a snoring body in a bed, "you are needed on the bridge." Auto then retreated to the bridge.

With no one else there but the sleeping Captain, WALL•E glanced around the dimly lit room. The walls were covered with portraits of former captains, their years of service listed beneath their names. The date under the first portrait was 2105. That was seven centuries ago, when the *Axiom* had been launched from Earth for its five-year cruise. It was now 695 years behind schedule for its return.

The captains had changed over time, growing larger and flabbier. Like the humans on the ship, the captains had declined, each one visibly less spirited than his or her predecessors.

The current captain reached out to quiet his alarm and accidentally pushed a button on WALL•E's chest instead. WALL•E cringed. The music of *Hello, Dolly!* blasted from his speaker.

The Captain flopped around in his bed, flustered. "All hands on deck!" he muttered. "What? Who? Who's there?" he asked, only half awake.

Luckily for WALL•E, a group of prep-bots filed into the room . . . and he found the Off button for the music. A beautician-bot, a massage-bot, and a wardrobe-bot surrounded the Captain's bed, which converted into a chair as the robots obediently brushed, massaged, and dressed the groggy human.

WALL•E tried to blend in by rubbing the Captain's feet. He accidentally tickled the Captain, making him giggle. Fortunately, WALL•E remained unnoticed, and he decided it was best to simply hide under the Captain's chair.

"Oh, you look gorgeous!" the beautician-bot said. The Captain nodded as his hover chair glided up toward the bridge. WALL•E clung to the under-side of the Captain's chair. The hover chair would take him back to the bridge—and EVE.

On the ship's bridge, Auto stood at attention, awaiting the arrival of the Captain. With a whir from his hover chair, the Captain finally entered the bridge. A coffee-bot rose from the console as WALL•E scooted out of sight.

"Sir," Auto said, unblinking.

"Coffee," the Captain demanded, heading for the large console.

Auto tried again. "Sir, the annual—"

The Captain held his hand up in Auto's direction. Trying to maneuver his large body, he adjusted his chair and was almost able to reach the coffee cup. "Protocol, Auto. First things first," he said, finally grabbing the cup and taking a sip.

The Captain was in no hurry. There was no

need for anyone to navigate the huge star liner. The *Axiom* had been in a holding pattern around Earth's galaxy for seven hundred years. At this stage, Auto controlled the ship far more than the Captain did.

The Captain's chair slowly followed a red line around the console. Panels lit up as he passed. "Mechanical systems?" the bored Captain asked the ship's computer.

"Unchanged," the computer answered.

"Reactor core temperature? Passenger count? Regenerative foodstuffs? Jacuzzi temperature? Waste flow? Laundry-service volume? Buffet menu?"

"Unchanged, unchanged, unchanged," the computer responded. The Captain's workday was over. He was about to order up the buffet when he glanced at the time. He flashed Auto a look. It was past noon!

"Sir, the annual recon—" Auto started. Auto wanted to tell the Captain about EVE.

"Twelve-thirty? Auto, you let me sleep in again!" the Captain complained.

"Sir—" Auto began. But the Captain snapped like a slingshot across to the bridge's lido deck side, his voice booming out over the passengers.

"The morning announcements," the Captain said. He turned a dial on the console and cranked the sun from midday back to sunrise. He smiled smugly. Now he hadn't overslept. Auto rolled his huge eye.

On the lido deck, passengers' lunch drinks were automatically switched to breakfast drinks, but no one seemed to care.

The Captain now appeared on every passenger's screen. A section of the fake sky became a large video display broadcasting his image.

"Good morning, ladies and gentlemen," he said in the competent voice of an experienced pilot. "Welcome to day 255,600 of the *Axiom*'s five-year cruise." It was the seven hundredth anniversary of the *Axiom*'s launch into space!

The Captain cheerfully announced that each passenger would receive a free cupcake to celebrate the occasion.

The Captain paused, noticing a flashing button on the console. "Hey? Hey, Auto, what is that flashing button? Auto?" he said, his microphone still on. "What the—?" Luckily, the microphone finally turned off.

Inside the bridge, the Captain had finally noticed EVE. Auto was reactivating her.

From under the console, WALL•E saw EVE return to life! Her white egglike shell was glowing again, and her soft blue eyes slowly opened.

"Eee-vah!" he said joyfully. WALL•E had caught up with EVE at last, and she was awake—alive!—again. Of course, he wasn't sure what he would do next. But at least he was with his true love!

CHAPTER 15

All business, EVE saluted the Captain. She was fully prepared to complete her directive—the secret directive she had refused to tell WALL•E about back on Earth.

The Captain stared at her. He noticed the green light flashing on her chest. It matched the green light flashing on his console. Not knowing what any of it meant, the Captain pushed the console button, just to see what would happen. The room suddenly went dark, and a holo-graphic screen displaying the image of BnL's CEO appeared.

"Greetings and congratulations, Captain!" the CEO declared brightly. "If you're seeing this, that means your Extraterrestrial Vegetation Evaluator, or 'EVE' probe, has returned from Earth with a

WALL•E is short for "Waste Allocation Load Lifter, Earth class."

WALL•E likes to examine the curious objects he finds in the trash.

WALL•E is intrigued when he finds a plant.
He has never seen one before.

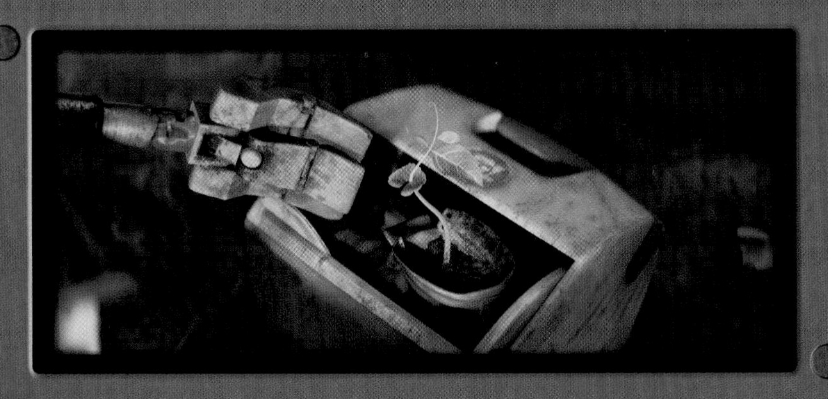

WALL•E carefully packs the plant and takes it
back to his truck.

WALL•E sees a glowing red dot on the ground. It's a laser beam.

WALL•E lifts his head out of the sand to take a peek at the spaceship.

A spaceship lands near WALL•E's truck.

A robot emerges from the ship. She is
a sleek new probe-bot.

WALL•E is smitten with the probe-bot.
Her name is EVE.

When WALL•E shows EVE his plant,
she takes it away from him.

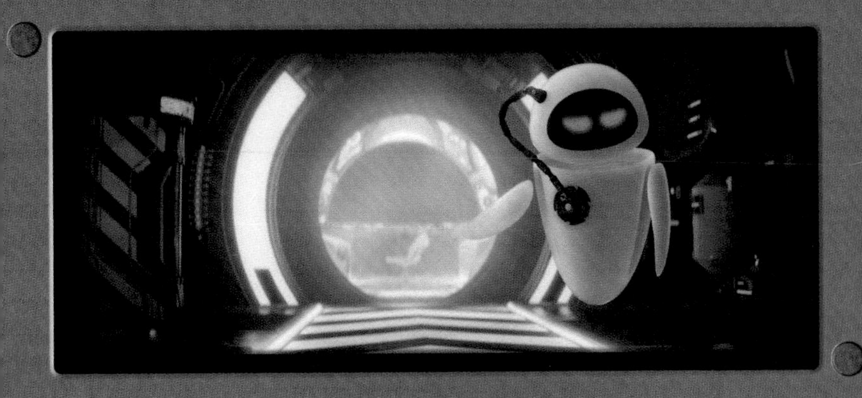

WALL•E follows EVE to a giant spaceship.
EVE tries to send him home in a life pod.

WALL•E takes a bumpy ride in the life pod!

WALL•E inspects the console in the life pod.
He wants to go back to EVE.

WALL•E and EVE prove that even robots
can fall in love.

confirmed specimen of ongoing photosynthesis.

"That's right," the CEO declared. "It means it's time to go back home!"

"Home?" the Captain said blankly to Auto. "Does he mean *home* home?"

Auto turned slightly, hardly acknowledging the question, as the CEO told them, "Now that Earth has been restored to a life-sustaining status, by golly, we can begin *Operation*: *Recolonize*!" An ancient, dusty manual slid out of the console. The Captain took it and blew the dust from its cover as the CEO continued: "Simply follow this manual's instructions to place the plant in your ship's holo-detector, and the Axiom will immediately navigate your return to Earth. It's that easy!"

The Captain looked at the manual again. The ship's holo-detector was out on the lido deck. If he just had to activate the holo-detector and put the plant in it, why bother with the manual, especially since it didn't seem to be working?

He couldn't find a button on it anywhere.

The CEO's message continued: "Now, due to the effects of microgravity, you and your passengers may have suffered some slight bone loss. But I'm sure a few laps around your ship's jogging track will get you back in shape in no time."

The overweight Captain looked confused. "We have a jogging track?" he asked Auto.

"Seriously," the CEO's recorded voice said, brimming with confidence. "If you have any further questions, just consult your operation manual." He flashed a big white BnL smile and said, "See you back home, real soon!"

The transmission ended. The stunned Captain held up the manual. He paused for a moment, not knowing what to do with it. Finally, he gave a command to it: "Operate!" Nothing happened.

Auto took the manual, opened it, and returned it to the Captain.

"Oh . . . will you look at that!" the Captain said. It had been a long time since he had read more than a simple line or two on a video screen. It had been even longer since any human had picked up a book and actually read it. "Oooh, that's a lot of words!"

As the Captain and Auto tried to read the manual, WALL•E couldn't resist moving closer to EVE. He tapped her on the shoulder. "WALL•E!" she exclaimed.

He gave her a tiny wave. But EVE worried that he might interfere with her directive, so she beeped and gestured for him to hide and stay quiet.

WALL•E just stared, thinking every sound and movement she made was simply amazing. "Eee-vah!" he sighed.

Auto and the Captain turned their attention back to EVE. "Well, let's open her up," the Captain said, humming a tune from *Hello, Dolly!* He didn't realize that he was remembering the music he had awakened to, the music that had come from WALL•E. He liked that song.

"Do you know what that song is?" he asked Auto. "It's been running through my head all morning."

EVE stood at attention, ready to present the plant that would complete her directive and start the process of sending the *Axiom* back to Earth.

But when she opened her storage compartment, it was empty. The plant was gone!

The Captain looked at Auto. "Where's the . . . thingie?"

"Plant," Auto replied.

"Plant. Right. Right," the Captain said. "Where is it?" He looked at the manual. "Maybe we missed a step," he said, thumbing through the pages. "Show me how you change the text again."

As Auto tried to help the Captain, EVE turned to WALL•E. "Plant! WALL•E!" she said impatiently. She thought he had taken the plant.

WALL•E looked back at her, wide-eyed.

"WALL•E!" she said sternly. She scanned his chest and found nothing. She picked him up and scanned the floor. Nothing was underneath. "Plant!" EVE demanded.

Confused and concerned, WALL•E scurried around, searching for the plant.

"Why don't you scan her, just to be sure?" the Captain said to Auto.

Auto reported a negative. "Contains no specimen," he told the Captain, and added, "Probe memory is faulty."

The Captain's excitement turned to disappointment. "So, then, we're not going to Earth?" he asked the unblinking eye.

"Negative," Auto replied.

The Captain nodded. "The probe must be defective. Send her to the repair ward."

Gopher immediately appeared from a pneumatic tube. He enveloped EVE in the energy bands used to restrain defective robots, then lifted her back into the transport.

"And have them run diagnostics. Make sure she is not malfunctioning," the Captain continued.

As EVE was carted off, the Captain finally saw WALL•E alone on the floor. The Captain stared at him for a moment. WALL•E waved innocently and shook the Captain's hand happily. "And fix that robot as well," the Captain ordered, as he wiped his hand, soiled by WALL•E's handshake. "Have it hosed down, or something. It's filthy."

As WALL•E and EVE were placed back in the transport, the Captain remained on the bridge, thumbing through the manual. "'. . . And the internal gyroscope will level out,'" he read, intrigued by the real workings of space travel.

He looked at his hand and noticed the filthy reminder of WALL•E's handshake. Reaching to clean it off, he paused, then took a sample and placed it on the console. Seconds later, the dirt was suspended in a beam of light.

The holo-screen showed pictures of dirt, and a computer voice announced, "Analysis: soil, dirt, or earth."

The Captain was curious. His eyes drifted toward a holo-graphic globe on a shelf. "Define 'earth,'" he told the ship's computer.

"Earth," it responded, as the beauty of forests and rolling green hills appeared on the screen. "The surface of the world as distinct from the sky or sea."

"Define 'sea,'" the Captain said, fascinated.

Great foaming blue waves suddenly appeared on his screen. The Captain was spellbound. In his relentless pursuit of EVE and true love, WALL•E was slowly affecting those around him. Even the Captain was showing interest in something. Like Mary, he was noticing a whole new world. He was enjoying being engaged in something beyond a digital experience.

At that same moment, WALL•E and EVE were being shuttled through the transport tunnel. WALL•E tried to catch EVE's eye, but she refused to look at him.

WALL•E and EVE were taken into the chaos of the ship's huge repair ward. Malfunctioning robots, confined by energy bands, chatted noisily and behaved wildly. Not realizing that they were defective, the bots tried to continue with their directives, making quite a scene. WALL•E spotted an overanxious massage-bot tearing a crash-test dummy to bits. In a corner, a mad defibrillator-bot was wildly waving his paddles, zapping at anything within his reach.

An orderly locked a red "defect" device onto EVE's head. These nonremovable devices made it difficult for the bots to escape the repair ward. The orderlies started toward WALL•E with one of the devices, but he dodged and escaped before they could tag him. His goal was to get away and save EVE.

And then . . . he was snatched by a defective beautician-bot, who slapped makeup onto his face. She held a mirror up and shouted, "You look gorgeous!"

Now thoroughly confused, WALL•E finally got caught in the robotic arms of one of the orderlies. The robot secured him to a spot along the wall.

WALL•E was locked down between a paint-bot, who was spraying paint everywhere, and a defective vacuum-bot, who was sneezing dust into WALL•E's face. It was not the best place to be locked down.

Rotating his head to peer past his two new companions, WALL•E watched the orderlies take EVE to be inspected. He could see her outline through the frosted glass of the diagnostic room.

WALL•E heard a defective bot howling somewhere in the repair ward. He was sure it was EVE. And he was sure they were hurting her!

A surge of energy rushed through WALL•E's circuits. Desperate to save her, he used the laser beam between his eyes to cut himself free. He fell to the ground, landing on his Play button. The same *Hello, Dolly!* song that had awakened the Captain earlier now blared across the repair ward. Every reject-bot froze. They all turned toward WALL•E. Stunned, they watched him crash through the glass doors and grab EVE's blaster arm, which the technician-bots had just removed.

WALL•E was trembling, but the message to the orderlies was clear: *Let her go, or else!*

The orderlies sprang at WALL•E, and in a moment of bumbling panic, he fired EVE's blaster. Fortunately, he was holding the blaster backward. The shot went wild, shattering the repair ward's control panel to smoking bits.

The blue energy bands around the reject-bots instantly disappeared. The trembling rejects were released! They stared for a moment and then cheered wildly.

EVE glared at WALL•E. He realized she had not been hurt after all. But now she certainly was angry.

"WALL•E!" she said sternly as a mob of excited rejects raced toward him. They lifted WALL•E onto their shoulders and carried their hero out of the ward. EVE followed, astonished, as sirens began to wail throughout the ship.

The escaping bots stampeded through the

halls. Umbrella-bots randomly opened and closed, and the paint-bot hurled paint in every direction. WALL•E helplessly bounced on top of the heap, still holding EVE's blaster arm.

A line of steward-bots appeared, blocking the reject-bots.

"Halt!" a steward barked.

WALL•E cowered. A small robot came forward and pushed his hero WALL•E closer to the stewards.

The reject-bots, anxiously awaiting the stewards' next move, suddenly saw EVE flying overhead. She swooped down, snatched her blaster arm, and yelled, "WALL•E!"

The steward-bots snapped their photo, and an image of WALL•E and EVE waving her dangerous blaster arm flashed across every screen in the *Axiom*.

"Caution!" the ship's computer announced. "Rogue robots! Rogue robots!"

Now they were really in trouble. WALL•E and EVE looked like criminals!

The stewards were preparing to lock WALL•E in a suspension beam when EVE snatched WALL•E up by his arm. She carried him high above their heads.

The reject-bots held back the steward-bots as EVE flew WALL•E through the crowded halls. She heard service robots shriek when they identified WALL•E and EVE as the blaster-arm-toting twosome on their screens. EVE looked for a place to hide.

She pushed WALL•E into an elevator. As it descended, their WANTED! image appeared on the elevator's screen. "Caution! Rogue robots!" blared on its speakers.

"Eee-vah!" WALL•E pointed excitedly to the picture of the two of them on the screen. He thought they looked a bit like the romantic couple in his favorite movie. But EVE realized that they looked like fugitives. She drew her arm back and blasted the screen to pieces.

WALL•E and EVE quietly entered the dark control room of the ship's emergency escape center. EVE found her way to the console that controlled the escape pods. She began tapping commands into the keyboard.

WALL•E glanced down at EVE's hand. He interlocked his own hands and thought that perhaps this was the right moment to take hers. "Eee-vah?" he said softly.

Before he could take her hand, the control console's lights blinked on and an escape pod appeared at the end of the room. Its hatch slowly tilted open.

EVE turned to WALL•E. "Earth," she said, pointing to an overhead screen. The screen displayed the coordinates of WALL•E's smoggy home planet.

She gestured for WALL•E to enter the pod, and the little robot rolled in. He looked back happily and patted the seat next to him. He was waiting for EVE to join him. But EVE wasn't moving. WALL•E gestured again for her to come, but she shook her head. She pointed to her chest and made her plant symbol glow.

"Directive," she said. She would stay behind to complete her directive.

As soon as WALL•E realized she wasn't going with him, he raced out of the pod and boxed up.

EVE sighed. She wanted WALL•E to go home and be safe. Then she could complete her directive without all the trouble he was causing her. She picked him up and carried him back into the pod. WALL•E raced out and tried to hide behind the console.

"WALL•E," EVE said, staring impatiently at the love-struck robot.

The chime of the elevator interrupted their standoff. Someone was coming!

EVE quickly shut down the control panel and retreated into the shadows with WALL•E. They heard something motor into the room, but it was too dark to see what it was.

An arm rose up to the console, and a robotic hand worked the keyboard. The lights blinked back on. In the glow, WALL•E and EVE saw . . . Gopher. The two bots exchanged a confused glance as Gopher removed something from his chest panel and placed it in the pod.

It was the plant! Shocked, EVE realized that Gopher had been working against her all along. He must have taken the plant from her while she was shut down.

WALL•E gazed at EVE. Now there was proof that he hadn't taken the plant from her! EVE acknowledged this with a sheepish shrug. She looked up to see Gopher returning to the console. He tapped another series of buttons.

When she turned back to WALL•E, he was gone. "WALL•E?" she whispered. He was inside the pod, trying to retrieve the plant for her.

"WALL•E!" she whispered again, calling him back. But just then, Gopher hit the launch button. *Whoosh!* The escape pod was instantly jettisoned into space. EVE watched as the plant—and WALL•E—slipped away from her.

As Gopher exited the room, EVE rushed to an air lock. She squeezed herself in and, with the push of a button, hurled herself into space.

Inside the escape pod, a terrified WALL•E was plastered against the rear wall. When the computer reported that the pod had reached cruising speed, WALL•E and the plant dropped to the floor.

"You may now turn on all electrical devices," the computer said.

WALL•E tried to get his bearings. He looked out the hatch and saw the *Axiom* getting smaller and smaller in the distance.

He made his way to the pilot's seat and pulled back hard on the lever. Nothing happened.

Frantically, he pushed all the buttons on the console at the same time.

Lights flashed. Oxygen masks dropped from the ceiling. The windshield wipers activated, and missiles deployed from the sides of the ship.

WALL•E kept pushing buttons. Then he hit the wrong one—the self-destruct button. "Pod will self-destruct in ten seconds," the computer said calmly. "You are now free to move about the cabin. Ten, nine, eight . . ."

WALL•E panicked. Desperately looking around for an escape, he saw a fire extinguisher and an emergency exit lever on the hatch. Hoping for the best, he grabbed the fire extinguisher and yanked the lever hard. Instantly, he was sucked into space as the pod exploded in a ball of fire beneath him.

EVE saw the escape pod blow up in the distance.

"WALL•E," she moaned, stunned. She had only meant to send the little robot home, not disintegrate him!

Suddenly, WALL•E whooshed by her. He was alive! Propelled by the fire extinguisher, he was heading right back toward the *Axiom*.

EVE turned and caught up to him.

Proudly, WALL•E opened his chest compartment and showed EVE the plant. He had saved it! EVE was delighted. She leaned toward WALL•E and a spark of energy—a robot kiss—passed between their heads.

Soon they were flying, side by side, making figure eights in perfect unison.

Inside the ship, Mary was staring out the window. She saw WALL•E and EVE dancing among the silver-white stars. "Oooh!" the human said excitedly.

Just then, John's hover chair drifted by. Mary reached out and turned off the electronics on John's armrest. He blinked and looked around.

"Hey!" Mary shouted at him. "Hey, look!"

She pointed to the window. "Look at that!" she hollered, startling John.

“Wha—!” He looked all around him. “Huh?”

Confused without his electronics, John glanced at Mary, and then out the ship’s window, which displayed a glorious view of the galaxy. Like Mary, he immediately saw WALL•E and EVE gliding through space, as if they were dancing on the stars.

“Oooh!” John exclaimed in awe. He recognized that little bot.

Both Mary and John drew closer to the window to watch. After the moment had passed, John reached down to his armrest to turn his electronics back on. But Mary’s hand was still there. The two hands touched. John turned to Mary, and their eyes actually met.

“Hi,” John said, and smiled.

“Hi,” Mary answered, smiling, too.

Up on the ship's bridge, Auto lazily watched the lido deck's sky turn from day to evening. Just below him, in the Captain's quarters, a computer was flashing images to the Captain one after the other.

"Define 'hoedown'!" the Captain told the computer.

The computer responded, "Hoedown: a special gathering at which lively forms of dancing would take place."

The Captain slapped his knee, enjoying every bit of Earth information he could get his chubby hands on.

The ceiling portal suddenly opened and Auto descended to face the Captain. The Captain looked up.

"Auto!" he exclaimed. "Earth is amazing!" He highlighted images on his computer as he spoke. "These are called farms!" Auto turned a bored eye to the screen as the Captain showed him fields of wheat and orchards of apples. "Humans would put seeds in the ground, pour water on them, and they would grow food, like pizza!"

Auto shut the screen. "Goodnight, Captain," he said, rising back to the bridge. The lights in the Captain's quarters went dark. Auto was telling the Captain that it was time to go to bed.

"Pssst," the Captain whispered to his computer. He was like a child who wanted to stay up to play. Only, in this case, the Captain wanted to know more about Earth. "Define 'dancing.'"

"Dancing," the computer began. At that moment, just outside the Captain's window, WALL•E and EVE spiraled around each other. "A series of movements involving two partners, where speed and rhythm match harmoniously with music."

Indeed, WALL•E and EVE were dancing. And, in a way, the Captain was dancing, too—at least in his mind.

Outside the *Axiom,* WALL•E's fire extinguisher spurted out its last bit of foam. He floated freely for a moment; then EVE took him in her arms to return him to the ship. To WALL•E, this was a dream come true.

Back inside the *Axiom,* EVE slowly led WALL•E down the corridors, trying to get to the Captain. A group of stewards passed by. The computer warned, "Caution! Rogue robots!" EVE pulled WALL•E aside to hide.

How could EVE get to the bridge to deliver the plant to the Captain?

CHAPTER 20

A towel cart—with EVE and WALL•E hiding behind it—slowly moved across the lido deck as the ship's announcer said, "Attention, passengers. The lido deck is now closing." Beach umbrellas suspended over hover chairs snapped shut, and the last few passengers glided out of the pool area. They were all dressed in blue except for the two wearing red in the pool.

"Hey now, stop that!" John said, laughing as Mary splashed at him.

"Make me," she answered playfully.

"Oh! Okay." John giggled and splashed her back.

A lifeguard-bot moved down from his tower. "No splashing! No diving!"

"Ahh! Switch off!" John yelled back, splashing the annoying robot. The lifeguard-bot short-circuited and toppled over, knocking a passenger into the pool.

"Whoa!" the man yelled as he fell into the water.

"Hang on!" Mary shouted as she and John each grabbed one of the man's arms. "We've got you!" Together they managed to lift the man out of the pool and back into his chair.

The man didn't know what to say. He, too, was unused to being without his electronic devices. He was actually looking at other human beings face to face, not over some holo-screen.

"Uh . . . thank . . . you?" he tried.

"You're . . . uh . . . welcome," John said, smiling.

The towel cart rolled by with WALL•E and EVE silently and carefully pushing it forward as it hid them from view. They could look up and see the Captain's quarters and the bridge. They were close now.

WALL•E peeked out and saw a line of stewards filling the lobby that led to the bridge. He quickly reversed the towel cart into the shadows. EVE scanned the area, searching for another way up to the bridge.

The trash chute! EVE realized that the chute went straight up to the bridge! She raised her hand, motioning to WALL•E to stay. He shook his head in protest. But EVE looked at him and said, "Waaaleeee," just as she had done when they first met. WALL•E tilted his head and sighed. Before he knew it, he found himself watching EVE zoom past the guards at superfast speed—and right up the chute.

Inside the Captain's quarters, a chubby hand moved a toy starship toward a holo-graphic globe. "Prepare for landing," the Captain said, inching the small model of the *Axiom* closer to the globe.

"We're here, everybody!" he announced to his pretend passengers. He walked his fingers over the globe and said in a high voice, "Yay, Captain! It's so beautiful!"

"No, it's nothing," he said, lowering his voice again. "I was pleased to do it. It's all about you people!"

A strange rattling interrupted his make-believe landing. The Captain turned away from the globe to see EVE rising from the trash chute.

EVE hovered in front of him, and to his

complete surprise, she opened her panel doors.

"The plant!" the Captain exclaimed. "How did you ever find it?"

EVE floated toward him and saluted. She presented him with the plant. He gazed at it in absolute wonder. "We can go home now!" he gasped. He looked at the holo-graphic globe. "What's it like now?" he asked EVE anxiously. "No, no, don't tell me," he said as he activated her memory chip, causing images from her mission to Earth to flash onto his screen.

The Captain squinted as the screen jumped from one scene to another. He watched EVE's journey through her eyes—all the things she had seen and recorded during her time on Earth.

But soon the Captain's happy anticipation evaporated. His brow furrowed as he saw images of Earth's terrible condition. These pictures were nothing like the ones he'd seen earlier on his computer. He began to worry. Earth was clearly too polluted. He couldn't guide his ship home to that mess. People would not be able to live there.

He looked down at the plant. A single leaf dropped. But wait—the Captain knew what to do. He had learned this from the computer. He would water the plant.

And as he turned to do so, he heard WALL•E's favorite song playing. EVE had recorded *Hello, Dolly!* when WALL•E had shown the video to her back on Earth.

"Hey, I remember that song!" the Captain said. And somehow it inspired him.

He looked at the plant. If this little guy could grow on Earth, then his passengers could grow and thrive there, too. By golly, they could even help clean up the planet and get rid of the pollution!

EVE continued to watch as her recording device kept playing back *Hello, Dolly!* She saw how WALL•E's favorite characters intertwined their hands. She looked down at her own hands and interlocked them. Suddenly, she understood what WALL•E had been trying to do. He had wanted to hold hands . . . just like the romantic couple in his movie.

Then EVE found herself watching images of the time on Earth when she had been dormant. She saw things she hadn't known about until now—images of WALL•E caring for her as she slept: WALL•E shielding her from the rain with his umbrella; WALL•E buried in a sandstorm, trying to protect her; WALL•E keeping watch day and night while she was shut down. She even saw him trying to jump-start her heart with his own.

"WALL•E," EVE said to herself, touched by the robot's selfless devotion. Finally, she realized that WALL•E loved her!

CHAPTER 22

Pacing back and forth outside the trash chute, WALL•E suffered through several changes of mind on how to take EVE's hand: upside down, sideways, from the left, or from the right.

WALL•E became more and more impatient. At last, he looked around for a disguise and spotted the towel cart. Covering himself in towels, he made his way to the trash chute's opening. Climbing inside, he began to crawl up the chute, using slow, crablike movements.

Meanwhile, in the Captain's quarters, EVE continued to watch images of WALL•E from her video recordings of Earth. She saw him etch their names in a heart. "WALL•E," she sighed.

The Captain was there, too. He turned to Auto,

holding the prized plant. "Auto," he said, "Probe One found the plant! Fire up the holo-detector!"

"Not necessary, Captain," Auto replied calmly. "You may give it to me."

The Captain held up a chubby finger. "You know what? I should do it myself!"

Auto shot over and blocked the Captain.

"Sir," Auto said sternly. "I insist that you give me the plant."

The Captain was shocked—and starting to get angry. Auto reported to him!

"Get out of my way," the Captain said firmly, trying to move past Auto.

"Sir, we cannot go home."

"What are you talking about, Auto? Why not?"

"That is classified," Auto said, leaning over the Captain. "Give me the plant!"

The Captain waved the plant around, out of Auto's reach. "What do you mean, 'classified'? You don't keep secrets from the Captain!"

"Give me the plant," Auto demanded.

"Tell me what's classified," the Captain snapped. "Tell me, Auto. That's an order!"

Auto finally punched a series of buttons with his robotic tentacle. A BnL message appeared on-screen. It was labeled TOP SECRET: FOR AUTOPILOT EYE ONLY.

The Captain watched as the face of BnL's leader appeared. Via the fuzzy old recording, the leader told the autopilots of all BnL star liners to take control of the ships and never return to Earth, as life there was "unsustainable."

"'Unsustainable'?" The Captain scoffed. He turned his gaze from the screen to the plant in his lap. For the first time, he had seen the truth: There was no great plan to return to Earth. His company and his leader had given up on him, his ship, and his passengers. The Captain's face grew red. He was holding living proof—the plant—that life was indeed sustainable on Earth. Now he was downright angry.

Auto held out one of his tentacled handles toward the Captain. "Now the plant."

"No!" the Captain shouted, refusing to give the plant to his autopilot. "This doesn't change anything, Auto! We have to go back!"

Auto had never expected this captain to defy him. But the Captain had finally come to the conclusion that if the little plant had grown and survived on Earth, so could the people on the *Axiom*.

"Sir," Auto answered, "orders are: Do not return to Earth."

"Because he thought nothing could survive there anymore," the Captain argued. "But that was hundreds of years ago! Now look at the plant—green and growing! It's living proof!"

"Irrelevant, Captain." Auto was sticking to his directive.

"What?" the Captain said, raising his voice. "No! It's completely relevant! Out there is our home. *Home*, Auto! And it's in trouble. I can't just sit out here and do nothing. That's all anyone's ever done on this blasted ship—*nothing*!"

"On the *Axiom*, you will survive," Auto answered mechanically.

The Captain's voice became stronger. "I don't want to survive! I want to *live*!"

Auto replied: "Must follow my directive."

The Captain turned away in frustration. Auto had slowly been taking over the Captain's rightful duties as leader of the *Axiom*, and it was for all the wrong reasons. The Captain turned back and stared at Auto. Then he looked down at the little plant in his lap.

"I'm the captain of the *Axiom*," he stated, filled with determination. "We are going home today!"

Auto gave off a series of electronic beeps, and Gopher instantly emerged onto the bridge. Gopher turned toward the Captain. A blue suspension beam suddenly lifted the plant from the Captain's hands.

"Hey, that's my plant!" the Captain yelled at Gopher. "This is mutiny!"

"Probe One," the Captain said to EVE, "arrest Auto!"

And then everything happened very fast. Gopher tossed the plant straight into the trash chute. The Captain gasped. This could not be happening! The plant was gone . . .

. . . until WALL•E appeared. Still climbing up the trash chute, he had caught the plant. He emerged from the chute, looking right at EVE, knowing she would be delighted.

Zzzzap! Auto electrocuted WALL•E. Just like that, the little bot fell to the floor, his circuitry fried. EVE—caught in one of Gopher's suspension beams—watched in horror as WALL•E was dumped down the trash chute.

Still in shock, EVE was barely aware as Gopher disabled her. The Captain gasped as Gopher's beam lifted EVE and unceremoniously threw her down the trash chute!

Turning to the Captain, Auto stated flatly, "You, sir, are confined to quarters."

The out-of-shape Captain was no match for Auto. Despite his attempts to resist, the Captain was pushed down into his quarters. The lights went out. He was now imprisoned without power or access to the outside.

Far below the Captain's quarters, WALL•E and then EVE crashed into the *Axiom*'s garbage bay. Tons of trash filled the room. The only light came from the faint orange glow of industrial lamps. Two giant compactor robots made a rumbling sound as they worked. WALL•A was emblazoned on their enormous square chests. They were Waste Allocation Load Lifters, *Axiom* class.

The giants each grabbed a ton of trash, cubed

it, and rotated. They stacked their massive trash cubes on a platform, and the cubes slid on rails into an air lock. The huge air-lock doors started to close with a hiss. Then the exterior hatch flew open, the vacuum of space instantly pulling out the cubed trash.

When EVE awoke, she realized that she and WALL•E were squashed tightly inside two of the giant trash cubes.

Quickly becoming alert, EVE understood the danger that she and WALL•E were in. If they did not get out soon, they would be lost forever in space. She struggled to break free from her trash cube, but she was too tightly wedged inside it. And then—*KA-BLAM!*—EVE used her blaster arm to blow up her trash cube and free herself. But WALL•E was still stuck in his cube.

To make matters worse, all the gigantic trash cubes were now inside the garbage bay's air lock. The outward pull was growing stronger and stronger. They were being sucked out into space!

Finally, EVE managed to pull WALL•E free. But the doors to the air lock were almost closed! M-O, the little cleaner-bot, was still obsessively following his directive, cleaning WALL•E's tracks all the way to the garbage bay. And as the doors were closing, M-O wedged himself between them, keeping them slightly ajar.

The giant WALL•As realized what was happening and moved over to open the doors. M-O was able to get back into the safety of the garbage bay. And EVE, pulling the injured WALL•E, barely made it out of the air lock and through the doors herself. The WALL•As and M-O had helped save WALL•E and EVE.

But WALL•E was badly hurt.

CHAPTER 24

Gently, EVE rested WALL•E against a pile of trash. Opening his chest, she saw that his circuitry had been burned by Auto's electric blast. She knew she had to do something fast, so she began searching in the garbage for a circuit board to replace WALL•E's ruined one.

M-O approached WALL•E. He gently began cleaning him, now as an act of friendship. All this time, M-O had been madly chasing WALL•E, intent on scrubbing him clean. Now he massaged WALL•E's metallic exterior with his softest brush. WALL•E had made M-O see the world differently, too.

EVE returned with a large selection of circuit boards. Then she reached out to hold WALL•E's hand—the one thing he had wanted from her all this time. But instead of giving his hand to her in return, WALL•E offered EVE the plant, which he had kept in his chest cavity.

Struggling to communicate, WALL•E insisted that EVE complete her directive. But EVE no longer cared about her job. She only cared about WALL•E. Tossing the plant aside, she began trying to repair him.

"Rrr." WALL•E struggled to say "Earth." EVE finally understood: If she wanted to repair him, she would have to get him back to Earth, to his home, where he kept all his spare parts.

EVE grabbed the plant. She no longer needed it to complete her directive. She needed it to make the *Axiom* return to Earth so that she could save WALL•E.

Quickly, she scooped up WALL•E and raised her blaster arm to the ceiling. There was a faster way out of this place, but it meant blowing a hole in one of the lower levels of the ship. *BOOM!*

M-O jumped on, too, as EVE flew WALL•E out of the trash bay.

Down in the robot service tunnel, the ship's stewards were feverishly trying to round up the escaped reject-bots, when the entire service hall began to shake. One steward was trying to stop the defective paint-bot from applying yellow lines to the floor. The paint-bot was confusing all the service-bots, who were trying to stay on their lines to follow their directives.

A low rumbling seemed to be coming from far below them. The steward was moving toward the noise when WALL•E, EVE, and M-O burst into the long corridor.

The steward sounded his alarm. He snapped a photo, focusing in on EVE and WALL•E . . . and the plant.

EVE, WALL•E, and M-O took off down the corridor with the paint-bot leaking paint behind them. The paint-bot was humming the song he remembered WALL•E playing in the repair ward.

That gave WALL•E an idea. Still weak and barely functioning, he managed to press the Play button on his chest. The tune echoed faintly through the hallway. But it was enough to lure the timid reject-bots out of hiding. Their hero had returned!

In only moments, the steward's photo had become a WANTED! poster. Images of EVE with WALL•E holding the plant flashed all over the ship. On the bridge, Auto saw the picture. He couldn't believe his eye. "Not possible," he moaned.

Below the bridge, locked in his quarters, the Captain noticed a flash on his computer screen. It was the EVE Probe, the dirty trash-compacting robot . . . and the plant!

The Captain's eyes lit up. A look of determination came over his face. He searched through the manual again and saw a picture of the holo-detector's activation button. Now he knew what he could do to help. He realized that he did not have to put the plant in the holo-detector to set the course for home. The EVE probe could do it without him.

He stared at the ceiling. Somehow, he had to get through that trapdoor and up to the bridge so that he could push the button.

The Captain rolled out of his hover chair, moved under his personal console, and started rewiring his computer. Soon his image and voice showed up on every holo-screen throughout the ship. He was sending a message to EVE.

"Pssst! Hey! Hey! This is the Captain. I'm locked in my room. Probe One, bring the plant to the lido deck. I'll have activated the holo-detector. Now, hurry! Auto's probably going to cut me off, and—"

The air was suddenly filled with static. But EVE and WALL•E had gotten the message. Instead of heading toward the Captain, they changed direction. They went up toward the lido deck . . . and the holo-detector.

EVE gently held WALL•E and dashed onto the next level, arriving at the courtyard of the economy-class deck. A wall of stewards came forward and tried to block their path. "Halt!" a steward shouted. Behind him, other stewards stood ready to use their freeze rays to stop WALL•E and EVE in their tracks.

The mob of reject-bots sprang into action. They would do anything for WALL•E. The defective beautician-bot lunged forward. Using her hand mirrors, she deflected the oncoming barrage of freeze rays. Umbrella-bots took up the cause and snapped open, protecting WALL•E, EVE, and the throng of reject-bots behind them.

On the bridge, Auto watched as the stewards'

blips disappeared from his screen. Certain that things couldn't get any worse, Auto was astounded to see the image of the Captain appear on his screen. And the Captain was holding the plant!

"Ha! Ha! Look what I got, Auto!" the Captain said, taunting him. "That's right! The plant!"

"Not possible," Auto answered angrily, his eye going wide.

The Captain was tricking Auto. He didn't have the real plant. He was merely projecting the image of the plant taken from EVE's memory chip into his hands.

"You want it?" the Captain said, hoping Auto would take the bait. "Come and get it, Blinky!"

The portal in the Captain's ceiling suddenly snapped open and Auto shot down into the room. Auto's eye saw nothing.

"Captain?" Auto said, cautiously searching the dark room. Suddenly, the Captain leaped at Auto. He grabbed on to the machine and refused to let go as Auto dragged him around the room.

"Let go! Let go!" Auto yelled. Auto thrashed wildly and finally yanked the Captain up through the portal in the ceiling and onto the bridge.

"You're not getting away from me, One-Eye!" the Captain shouted. He reached for the big blue button as he and Auto flailed around the bridge.

"That's it! A little closer," the Captain grunted. "Must . . . push . . . button!"

All of a sudden, Gopher popped out of his pneumatic tube and saw the fight. He immediately charged toward the Captain.

Auto whipped the Captain around, accidentally hitting Gopher with the Captain's foot. The force sent Gopher crashing through the control-room window. With his siren screaming, Gopher landed in a heap on the lido deck below.

EVE flew WALL•E through the economy-class level of the *Axiom*. The humming throng of reject-bots was happily following them. They still needed to get up to the lido deck, which was past the main concourse and the coach-class deck.

Then another crowd of stewards appeared. They launched a web of freeze rays, locking down WALL•E, EVE, and the reject-bots.

But the Captain was not giving up. Working harder than he had in his entire life, he struggled against Auto up on the bridge. Finally, still clinging to Auto, the Captain managed to get one hand free . . . and smacked the blue button.

"Ha! Ha! Gotcha!" the Captain yelled to Auto.

As the alarm sounded all over the ship, the

Axiom's automated systems prepared the passengers for their return flight to Earth. Hover chairs carrying passengers poured out of the guest suites.

The stewards toppled, crushed by the uncontrollable onslaught of hover chairs heading up to the lido deck. And when the stewards fell, their freeze rays dissolved, freeing WALL•E, EVE, and the reject-bots.

EVE quickly resumed course, cradling the weakened WALL•E. The reject-bots followed close behind. At last, they reached the lido deck.

A huge cylinder rose from the floor. It was the holo-detector.

The entire ship's population was gathering. Passengers lined the balconies on all sides, and the floor was filled to capacity.

The giant video screen in the fake sky flashed on. Everyone looked up and saw the Captain.

"Ladies . . . and gentlemen!" the Captain said, gasping as Auto knocked him into the console. "Remain seated. Just a slight delay. Stand by!"

The passengers were confused. Mary looked around and saw several toddlers in their hover rings. All the commotion had frightened them. She and John rushed over. They soothed the toddlers, then passed them to other passengers in hover chairs.

Above them, the huge video screen continued to broadcast the struggle between the Captain and Auto. Auto seemed to be getting the upper hand. The entire ship tilted to one side. Passengers tumbled from their chairs, but WALL•E managed to hold on to the holo-detector.

Pushed to the side of the ship, EVE saw a monorail car fall off its track. She looked around. Mary and many of the children were next to her. They were in the sliding monorail's path.

EVE needed to place the plant in the holo-detector. But she wanted to help the passengers, too.

EVE zoomed toward the monorail and, using both hands, held it back. The plant, now slipping away, was lost somewhere on the tilting deck. To make matters worse, sliding passengers piled up against the monorail, adding more weight as EVE struggled to hold the car up.

Up on the bridge, Auto kept the ship tilted.

Then he switched the holo-detector button off.

The leaning holo-detector began moving back down into the deck. WALL•E barely held on. He wedged himself under one side of the holo-detector, trying to keep it from closing up. The pressure squished WALL•E into a box. Damaged as he already was, WALL•E refused to give up.

From the bridge, Auto could see that the holo-detector was jammed. He saw WALL•E struggling against the hydraulics of the huge cylinder.

"No!" Auto cried.

The Captain watched helplessly as Auto repeatedly pushed the holo-detector button. Looking up at Auto's screen, the Captain saw WALL•E being crushed. The passengers were screaming as the tilting ship tossed them around.

The Captain grasped the console's rails and pulled himself up to his wobbly feet. Standing, he looked around the control room. He'd never seen things from this position before.

Breathlessly, the passengers watched the giant screen. The Captain was actually standing! He took a step and then began to walk. The crowd cheered wildly.

Auto turned to see what the fuss was about and found himself face to face with the Captain. They had never been at eye level before. Auto stared, stunned, as the Captain lifted a finger . . . and turned off Auto's power. It was just that simple.

"Noooo," Auto moaned as his eye faded out for good. The Captain smiled triumphantly. The passengers roared, beaming with pride at their new hero.

The Captain took command of the bridge. He grabbed the ship's wheel and turned it. Passengers spilled across the lido deck as the *Axiom* leveled itself.

EVE set the monorail down and zoomed over to WALL•E. He was pinned under the edge of the holo-detector. She tried to lift it, but it wouldn't budge. It was still closing, crushing WALL•E in the process.

EVE looked for the plant. She knew that if the holo-detector closed, she would never be able to save WALL•E. Suddenly, from across the deck, she heard a robot calling out to her. It was M-O! He raised the plant for her to see from across the lido deck. EVE waved as M-O teamed up with the reject-bots, who worked with the humans to pass the plant to EVE. Every one of them had been inspired in some way by WALL•E.

EVE grasped the plant and fitted it—at the last possible second—into the sinking holo-detector.

The detector scanned the plant. "Plant origin identified," the ship's computer said. "Global reparation complete. Set course for Earth."

The lido deck's sky suddenly became transparent, revealing the sea of stars floating in space. The passengers gasped, and one by one, they began to take in the world beyond their own tight confines. The red coordinates for Earth glowed against the darkness of outer space as the ship's computer announced, "Hyperjump in twenty seconds."

The holo-detector rose. EVE's directive had been completed. The *Axiom* would return to Earth!

But the happy moment was lost when WALL•E toppled out from underneath the holo-detector.

He was in even worse shape than before—badly crushed and leaking oil. EVE looked at him and gasped.

"WALL•E?" EVE said, trying to take his hand. But WALL•E was fading. His hand dropped from hers.

EVE hardly noticed as the ship's computer began the countdown: "Ten . . . nine . . . eight . . ."

She just tried to hold on to WALL•E as the *Axiom* jumped to its fastest speed. She had seen him repair himself with the spare parts in his home on Earth. She would take him there. And she would try to bring him back to life.

Up on the bridge, the stars streaked by and the delighted Captain steered the ship and held on for the high-speed ride to Earth.

CHAPTER 28

On the broken freeway overpass where his master had left him, WALL•E's lonely cockroach was still obediently waiting.

Suddenly, a red dot appeared on the ground. Gently at first, the ground began to shake. The little roach looked back at the sky. A dark shape was growing, blotting out the sun. Slowly, the giant keel of the *Axiom* broke through the clouds, throwing the entire landscape into shadow.

Hundreds of glowing red dots rushed past. The excited cockroach could sense that his master was close to home and eagerly chased after the dots. Above him, the sleek city-sized star liner gracefully descended from the sky.

The earth shuddered. Towers of trash tumbled

as the *Axiom* set down, home at last.

A row of giant doors on the side of the ship slid open. Multiple gangways extended from each doorway to the ground.

The Captain was the first to take a tentative step outside the ship. The other passengers stood at the tops of the gangways, unwilling to leave the ship. They looked out at Earth's skyline for the first time.

"I don't know about this," one passenger said.

"Can't we stay on the ship?" said another.

The crowd grew nervous, hurling questions at the Captain and one another. "We came eight million miles for this?" "Can they turn the lights down?" "It's getting kind of warm."

"At least it's a dry heat," one passenger noted.

Then EVE appeared. She flew outside, clutching WALL•E tightly in her arms. The reject-bots followed behind her. The battered, boxed-up little WALL•E unit was almost home.

EVE paused at the bottom of the gangway.

WALL•E's happy little cockroach saw his master . . . and realized that something was wrong. He rushed up and jumped onto EVE's back, inching close to WALL•E.

EVE looked out over the landscape. Scanning the vast dry bay, she spotted WALL•E's deserted truck. The sooner she could get to WALL•E's spare parts, the sooner she could fix him. She took to the sky and zoomed across the bay, with the reject-bots following below in the sludge, trying unsuccessfully to keep up.

WALL•E's treasures jingled on the shelves as the back door slowly opened. EVE flew in and set WALL•E on his back. She quickly scoured the rotating shelves and found WALL•E's collection of spare parts.

Using a rusty car jack, she ratcheted up WALL•E's crushed body and grabbed the spare parts. With sparks flying, EVE frantically began to repair WALL•E.

Finally, she placed new solar panels on

WALL•E, raised her blaster arm, and blew a hole in the truck's roof. A shaft of sunlight beamed down on WALL•E as EVE held her breath and watched. Would the solar rays give him the energy he needed?

The reject-bots, still trying to catch up with EVE, saw the explosion that erupted from WALL•E's truck. Back at the ship, the Captain also saw it. But he kept moving forward, carrying the plant. When he reached a spot of soil at the bottom of a gangway, he knelt down and began digging a hole. When he felt that it was deep enough, he gently placed his precious plant inside, carefully patting the soil in around the stem. It was one tiny plant, but it was a beginning.

Meanwhile, the reject-bots kept racing toward WALL•E's truck.

And inside the truck, EVE waited. At first, nothing happened. Then she heard one faint beep; then another. WALL•E's head slowly rose out of his box, and his big eyes blinked open. The cockroach jumped up and down. His robot master was alive!

EVE looked at WALL•E and held out her hand to him.

"WALL•E," she hummed softly.

But WALL•E didn't answer. He stared at her blankly. EVE pointed to herself, saying, "EVE, EVE." WALL•E looked at her for a moment, then rotated his head away.

This couldn't be happening! EVE tried to show WALL•E some of his favorite collections, but he didn't seem to care. He simply wanted to gather them like trash and compact them into cubes. He had become just another WALL•E unit, following his directive.

"No!" EVE cried, frustrated and angry, as she watched him roll outside. After all this time, all that WALL•E had done . . . how could he be gone, just a shell of his former self? It wasn't fair.

Sadly, EVE followed him outside and leaned her head against his. She closed her eyes and grieved because love, the real spark of life, had left his robot heart.

As EVE held WALL•E's hand—the only thing he had ever really wanted from her—a spark of energy passed between their heads—a robot kiss.

EVE felt WALL•E wiggle his hand. Looking into his eyes, she saw some light returning to them. He began to focus. His hand clasped hers more tightly.

She saw the real WALL•E's eyes blink to life.

"Eee-vah?" he said as his eyes widened.

"WALL•E!" she cried. The reject-bots had finally arrived, and now they cheered. The cockroach chirped happily.

And as WALL•E's favorite song played from inside his truck, another tiny arc of electricity sparked between him and EVE. WALL•E's moment had finally arrived. As he held EVE's hand, he felt her squeeze his in return.

As the sun set behind the *Axiom,* the Captain led the rest of his passengers down the ramp.

"C'mon, everyone," he said heartily. "It's one small step for man, one giant—" But before he could take the next step, his small feet went out from under him and he tumbled down the ramp.

A steward-bot chased after him, shouting, "Please remain stationary!"

The passengers watched as the stewards surrounded their captain. Straining, he raised himself to his feet.

"No, no, I'm all right, I can do it myself." The Captain didn't want any help. And as he stood and dusted himself off, the crowd was filled with a kind of pride that had long been forgotten.

"Okay," he said to his passengers, who were now eager to follow his lead. "We're going to dig the water well here." He pointed to the empty bay and took in the desolate horizon. "And dig the food well over there.

"Ahhh," he said, smiling, knowing that humans and their planet had been given another chance. "This is going to be great!"

The Captain was right. He and his passengers would soon find out that another change had taken place. Off on a distant mountain of trash, a green field of tiny plants was sprouting.

Across the bay, WALL•E and EVE sat on the roof of his truck, happily watching the sun set over planet Earth. WALL•E would never really understand how he had caused so much change just by following his heart. But holding hands with EVE, surrounded by a throng of joyful reject-bots, he knew that, finally, everything in the universe was as it should be.